The Letter E Leaves the Alphabet

The Letter E Leaves the Alphabet

Martha Lane
Illustrated by Deborah White

This is a book for children
And for the child
In all of us who still
Wants to be First!

The Letter E Leaves the Alphabet

© Martha Lane 2012

Published by
Lighthouse Christian Publishing
SAN 257-4330
5531 Dufferin Drive
Savage, Minnesota, 55378
United States of America

www.lighthousechristianpublishing.com

Introduction

The letter E was very angry. He was angry at his brothers and sisters. E was angry at his mom and dad. He wanted to move out of his home and live somewhere else. E no longer wanted be part of his family and he had very good reasons.

In his whole life he had never been first in the family line-up for anything because the family did everything in alphabetical order. E did not like living with such a large family. He didn't know anybody who had a family of twenty-six (26). Getting ready for bed was a nightmare. It took hours for baths, brushing teeth and prayers.

And mom and dad divided the family into consonants and vowels even putting vowels in alphabetical order. A, E, I, O, U, those who were born first, were called vowels and everybody else was called a consonant. E did not like being called a vowel. It reminded him of a towel, or the howl of a wolf. And if that was not bad enough, E could never, ever be first in the alphabet. His sister A was always first. Everybody thought A was an academic angel.

Every night E's mother or his father (they took turns), would read to all the letters. E waited for his mother's night to ask his question, because his mom said "yes" more than his dad did.

"Mom," said E, "I want to be the first letter in the alphabet."

His mother gasped and looked at him with shock. Then she

hugged him and called him her precious letter E, whispering in his ear, "The Letter Maker created you and decided where you should be in the alphabet; the Letter Maker thinks you are perfect and in exactly the right place and so do I," his mother explained.

Then his mother said, "Son, the Letter Maker, who thinks you are very special, put you in exactly the right space. Only the Letter Maker can take you out of your place in the alphabet.

E did not feel special and being out of his family is just what he wanted. Let's see...

What happened to the Letter E?

This book is dedicated to Eric who taught me how important it is to listen to children, to ask them what they think and to make sure each and every child gets a chance to be First.

In The Beginning

A long time ago,
    way back when
In a place between
    now and then
Something awesome appeared
    on the scene,

The Letter Maker
    created his dream,

A family of letters,
    twenty-six in all

Each in its place,
    some short, some tall.

They lived together for eons of time
Wrote books and songs and
    many a rhyme.

Then something strange
    took place
to time and life
and all   of space...

On a cold December day,
In his home, far away;

The letter E said that he
Was leaving the alphabet family.

E told his mom, he told his dad,
He told them all what made him mad.

E said it loud, he said it clear,
He shouted it for all to hear!

" I'm leaving if I cannot be
First in the alphabet family!"

He put on his coat,
gloves and hat,
And walked
out saying,
" That is that!"

Leaving a note
for the dog to reveal,
E drove away on his
snowmobile.

E's brothers and sisters, everyone,
Ran to tell what E had done,

"Mother, father, come and see,
We can't find the letter E.

We've looked high, we've looked low,
Where he is we do not know."

"Look in the house, look in the yard,
Call 911, call the National Guard!"

All the letters went back to their beds,
And pulled the covers over their heads.

Grandmom prayed and grandad, too,
And then they knew just what to do.

"Find the dog, get E's note,
Read every word he wrote."

The
~Note E Wrote~

"I do not want to be Fifth in the alphabet family.
Did everyone of you forget?
I'm the most used letter in the alphabet!

"I AB-SO-LU-TE-LY
work harder than all the ABCs.
Computers here, encyclopedias there,
Email, E-mail everywhere.

Nobody cares what I think.
Alphabetical order stinks!

I'm on a f-a-s-t delivery
In a truck marked with an E,

To ask the Letter Maker to change,
The way the alphabet is arranged.
I'm out of here, no more for me."
Signed,
THE ANGRY LETTER
E

All TV and radio station
Sent this message
to the nations:

-EMERGENCY-EMERGENCY-
We can't find the letter E.

If E decides to stay away
One whole night and one whole day,

Every E in every word
Will never again be seen or heard.

Computers will crash, e-mail will stop.
And from each word all E's will drop.

-EMERGENCY-EMERGENCY-
We can't find the letter E."

The President closed the schools.
Workers put down their tools.

Every library locked each door.
Printing presses
printed no more.

EMERGENCY
THE
LETTER E
!MISSING!

To the castle
E
did
flee...

... and got down on bended knee.

Letter Maker, good and true.
I have come to plead with you.

Change the way the letters stand,
I am the Super Letter Man.'

I want the alphabet to be
E-B-C-D-A not A-B-C-D-E.

A is always number one.
Everywhere we walk or run.

All students want an A
On their papers every day.

I want to be a 1st place winner.
I want to be first in line for dinner.

The Letter Maker looked at E
And spoke as kindly as could be.

Your mother told you long ago,
The Letter Maker made you so.
Twenty~six letters, one by one,
Vowels and consonants 'til it was done.

Vowels are the pals of the alphabet.
  Consonants sometimes regret,
That the vowels a, e, i, o, u
Are the alphabetical super glue.

A word is not a word, you know,
Without a vowel to make it so.

And you must be silent in a word
to help another vowel be heard

Especially in lake and take
    Shake,
      bake,
        make and
          cake."

The Letter E hung his head.
Then looked up and sadly said.
"It is not fair it is absurd
To be silent in any word."
"If I can never be First in this family,

The alphabet will become.
Twenty-six letters minus one.

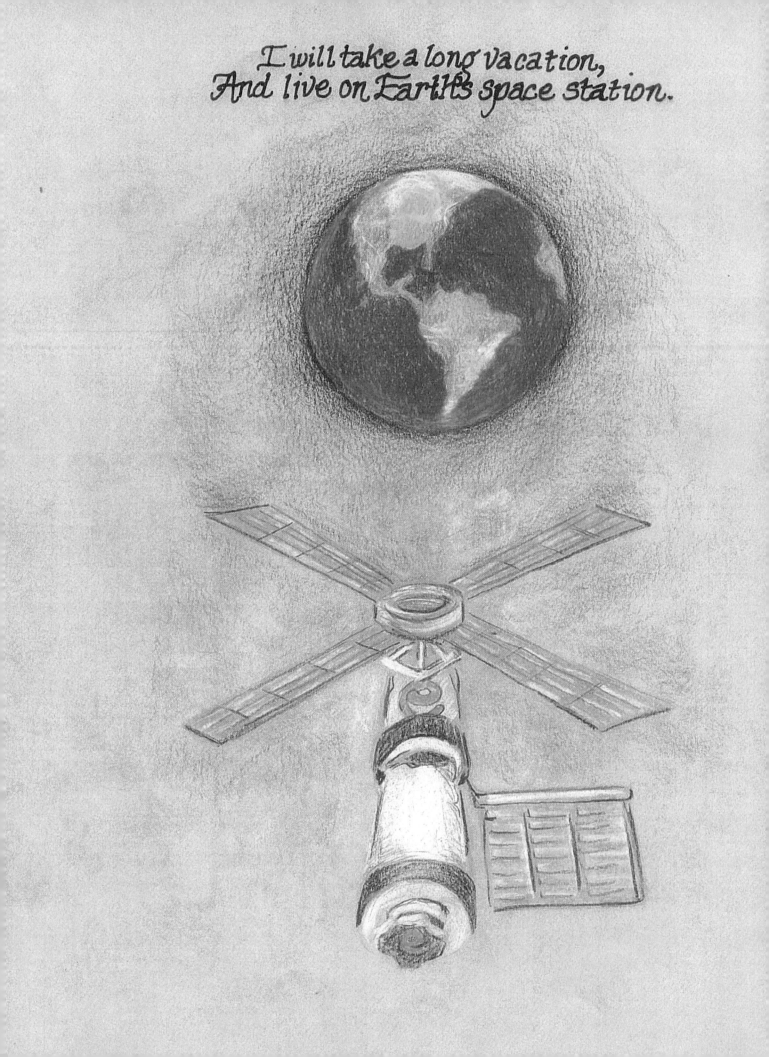

The Letter Maker said to E,
If you leave your family,
Every E in every word
Will fly away like a bird.
No one else can take your place.
you will leave an empty space.

You must decide, do it soon,
Or every single book is doomed.
Your family has come to let you know,
What would happen if you go?
Hear the things they never will do.
Hear what would happen without you."

"A will never answer the phone.
B can't give the dog a bone.

C will lose all her cheer.
D shall never see a deer.

F cannot fight a fire
Or help fix a flat tire.

G could never graduate
H can't help bears hibernate

I will never skate on ice,
Eat ice cream or roll the dice.

J shall never drive a jeep.
K will no secrets keep.

L can never love another.
M shall not become a mother.

N will stop being neat.

O no homework can complete.

P shall never pilot a plane.
Q will never be Queen again.

R can rake no fall leaves.
S will not be able to sneeze.

T will never climb a tree,
Play a tune, or count to three.

U cannot untie shoe laces
V will hold no flowers in vases.

W can never paint things white,
Ride a wave, or learn to write.

X knows exit signs will go.
And the word excellent also.

Y will never sing "Yankee Doodle,"
Yell a yell or eat a noodle.

Or Z can never zip a zipper
get a haircut with a clipper.

In a chorus the letters shouted!
"LETTER E ONLY YOU CAN DO
WHAT WAS CREATED JUST FOR YOU!
No matter where you stand,
You are the "Super Letter Man."

We can't rearrange, it must always be,
But you could change your heart and see,

That without YOU letter E,
We are not a family."

The Letter Maker dried E's tear
And whispered softly in his ear.

"Choose right now what you will do,
All of us are waiting for you."

The Letter E's Reply

Was shouted out to all the sky:
'My eyes are open. I now can see
Thank you family for loving me.

All the letters from A to Z
Are exactly where they need to be.

Nothing would ever be the same,
If in space I remain.
I see no one can take my place.
I truly want to keep my space.

You have made me happy today.

I am coming home to stay.

Letter Maker and family too,
Forgive me please. for leaving you.

Welcome Home

And so the alphabet family,
Lived happily ever after, with E.
THE END

The Story Behind the Story

This story grew from an incident which occurred during the first week of school, where I was the Director of a Before and After School Care Program.

Eric, a first grader, threw himself on the floor and started crying after his mother left the building. Helping him to his feet, we moved to a cafeteria table to talk. Looking for a way to comfort Eric, I asked him why he was crying. He picked up his head, wiped his tears and spoke these astonishing words, "I want to kill myself."

My immediate reactions were that he did not know what he was talking about and could not mean what he was saying. However, knowing these words should always be taken seriously, I did let the principal know what had happened.

"Why do you feel so sad?" I asked him. His words, "Because nobody ever listens to me, nobody cares what I think and I never get to be first," touched me deeply. I said "Eric, in this program you will always be first with me."

He successfully attended the Before and After Care School program for the next six years, often becoming my assistant. Eric was repeatedly drawn to the Block Center, where hundreds of wooden blocks of all shapes and sizes were available. He built four feet high apartments, complete with windows, three feet wide baseball stadiums and long winding highways. I began to see that Eric would make a wonderful architect and told him so.

I joyfully attended Eric's graduation from elementary school and proudly watched him receive his high school diploma. In June of 2011 Eric graduated from a state university where he received a degree in architecture. He is now employed by an architectural firm in the Mid West.

It is to the young boy named Eric, who has grown into a fine, talented young man, that I dedicate this book, "The Letter E Leaves the Alphabet." It is my hope and prayer that this story will help both the children and the adults who read the book to discover that they, like the letter E, are a one of a kind, irreplaceable treasure, with a purpose no one else can accomplish.